With thanks to Margery

for planting the seed of this idea

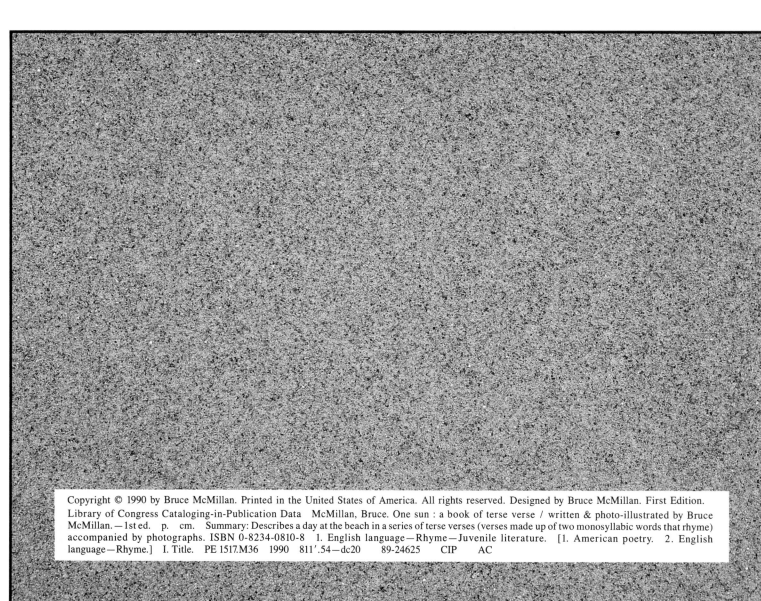

Copyright © 1990 by Bruce McMillan. Printed in the United States of America. All rights reserved. Designed by Bruce McMillan. First Edition.
Library of Congress Cataloging-in-Publication Data   McMillan, Bruce. One sun : a book of terse verse / written & photo-illustrated by Bruce McMillan. — 1st ed.   p.   cm.   Summary: Describes a day at the beach in a series of terse verses (verses made up of two monosyllabic words that rhyme) accompanied by photographs. ISBN 0-8234-0810-8   1. English language — Rhyme — Juvenile literature.   [1. American poetry.   2. English language — Rhyme.]   I. Title.   PE 1517.M36   1990   811′.54 — dc20   89-24625   CIP   AC

ONE SUN

A BOOK OF TERSE VERSE

WRITTEN &
PHOTO-ILLUSTRATED BY

BRUCE McMILLAN

HOLIDAY HOUSE   NEW YORK

SAND

HAND

LONE
STONE

SNAIL

TRAIL

SIX
STICKS

SMALL

BALL

WET

PET

NEAT

SEAT

STUCK

TRUCK

WHALE

PAIL

SCOOP

GROUP

ROUND

MOUND

PINK

DRINK

WHITE
KITE

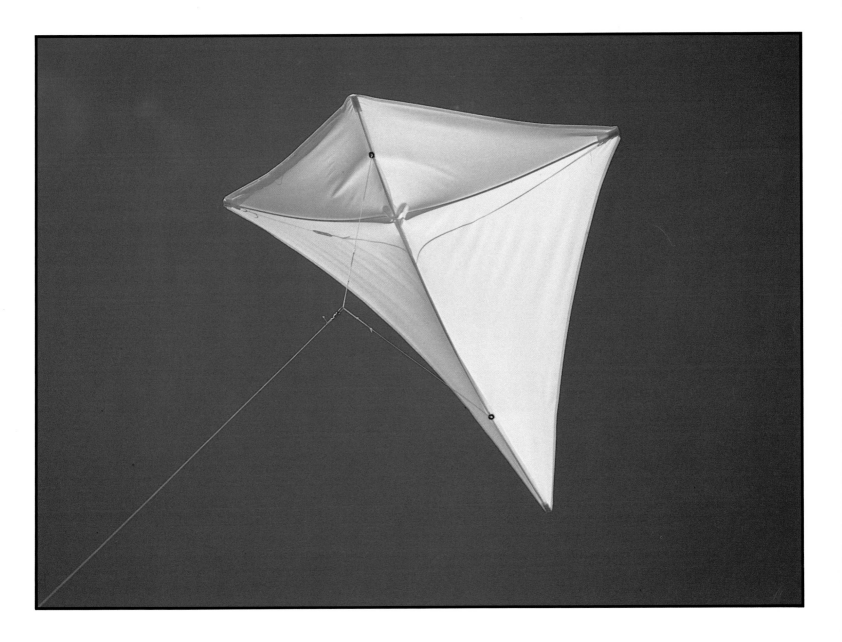

A *"snug tug"* on a *"string thing"* in a *"green scene"*

A terse verse is made up of two monosyllabic words that sound alike. They don't have to be spelled similarly, but they do have to <u>sound</u> alike. Getting children to make up their own terse verses is a delightful and stimulating way of introducing them to rhyme.

One Sun shows a day of play at the beach, but children can make up their own rhyming word pairs about anyplace or anything. For example, children might find a *"big twig"* or see a *"third bird"*! They might still be thinking of terse verses as they fall asleep in a *"red bed"*.

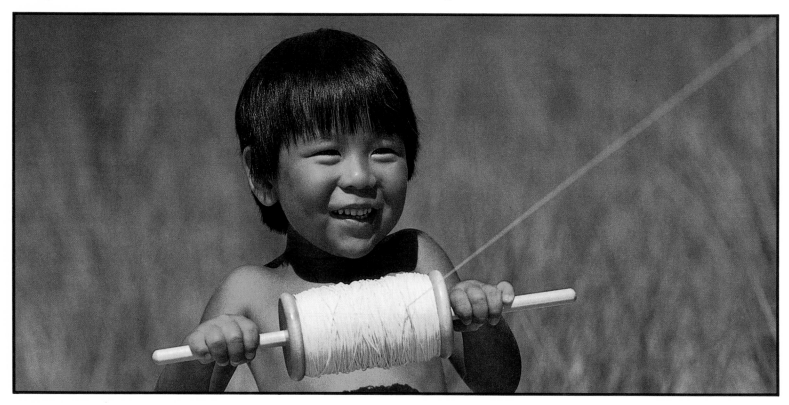

My young friend, Brandon Seavey, was photographed playing at the beaches of York County, Maine. He is the *"one son"* of Betsy, a first-grade teacher, and Stedman Seavey. Also photographed were blue-suited Stacey Bradbury, red-suited Billy Chace, yellow-suited Laura Reid, lifeguard Greg Sturman, and *"wet pet"* Scooby Joyal.

After selecting and coordinating the colors of the bathing suits and props, this book was photo-illustrated using a Nikon F4 with 20mm, 24mm, 50mm, 55mm Micro, 85mm, or 180mm Nikkor lenses; a circular-polarizing filter or blue color-correcting filter; and a reflector to lighten the shadows. The film used was Kodachrome 64 processed by Kodalux.